Hot fox

by Dick Crossley
illustrated by Sue King

introducing the short o sound,
as in hot

Fox went box, box, box.

Contents

Cover illustration by Sue King

A catalogue record for this book is available from the British Library

Published by Ladybird Books Ltd
80 Strand London WC2R 0RL
A Penguin Company

6 8 10 9 7

© LADYBIRD BOOKS LTD MM

LADYBIRD and the device of a Ladybird are trademarks of Ladybird Books Ltd

Printed in China

He went hop, hop, hop.

Fox went jog, jog, jog, up to the top.

Are you too hot, Fox?

nod nod nod

Yes, Ill have some pop!

bob bob bob

Tom's dog

by Mandy Ross
illustrated by Rosalind Beardshaw

more on the short **o** sound,
as in dog

Tom's dog has
lots of spots.

Tom and Bob do
not have spots.

Now Tom and Bob have
lots of spots,

and Tom's dog has
not got spots.

Snug
as a bug

by Mandy Ross
illustrated by Marjolein Pottie

introducing the short **u** sound,
as in bug

Here is a bug and

here is a rug.

Here is a bug in a rug.

Here is a bug who is snug in a rug. Goodnight!

Yum yum!

by Dick Crossley
illustrated by Karl Richardson

more on the short **u** sound,
as in mud

Take a mug of bugs,

a jug of slugs,

and a c p of m d.

Put it all in a tub and mush it up.

20

Yum! Yum!

Lunch is fun!

The Tip Top Chip Shop

by Richard Dungworth
illustrated by Sami Sweeten

introducing the ch sh
and th sounds

This is the Tip Top
Fish and Chip Shop.

This is the man who
chops the chips...

at the Tip Top
Fish and Chip Shop.

He chops thin chips, thick chips, lick your lips chips.

I like chips.

I wish I had a big dish of fish and chips.

I want thin chips, thick chips, lick your lips chips.

So I will dash with my cas
to the Fish and Chip shop.

For my thin chips, thick
chips, lick your lips chips.

phonics

Learn to read with Ladybird

phonics is one strand of Ladybird's **Learn to Read** range. It can be used alongside any other reading programme, and is an ideal way to support the reading work that your child is doing, or about to do, in school.

This chart will help you to pick the right book for your child from Ladybird's three main **Learn to Read** series.

Age	Stage	Phonics	Read with Ladybird	Read it yourself
4-5 years	Starter reader	Books 1-3	Books 1-3	Level 1
5-6 years	Developing reader	Books 2-9	Books 4-8	Level 2-3
6-7 years	Improving reader	Books 10-12	Books 9-16	Level 3-4
7-8 years	Confident reader		Books 17-20	Level 4

Ladybird has been a leading publisher of reading programmes for the last fifty years. **phonics** combines this experience with the latest research to provide a rapid route to reading success.

he fresh, quirky stories in Ladybird's twelve
phonics storybooks are designed to help your
child have fun learning the relationship between letters,
r groups of letters, and the sounds they represent.

his is an important step towards independent
ading – it will enable your child to tackle new words
r 'sounding out' and blending their separate parts.

How phonics works

- The stories and rhymes introduce the most
  common spellings of over 40 key sounds,
  known as **phonemes**, in a step-by-step way.

- Rhyme and alliteration (the repetition of an
  initial sound) help to emphasise new sounds.

- Coloured type is used to highlight letter groups,
  to reinforce the link between spelling and sound:

    ## and the King sang along.

- Bright, amusing illustrations provide helpful
  picture clues, and extra appeal.

How to use Book 3

The stories in Book 3 introduce your child to two of the five short vowel sounds—o as in fox and u as in mud—and the ch, sh and th sounds. They will help your child begin reading simple words containing these sounds.

⬤ Read each story through to your child first. Having a feel for the rhythm, rhyme and meaning of the story will give her* confidence when she reads it for herself.

⬤ Have fun talking about the sounds and pictures together. What repeated sound can your child hear in each story?

⬤ Help your child break new words into separate sounds (eg. h-o-t) and blend them together to say the word.

⬤ Point out how words with the same written ending sound the same. If b-ug says 'bug', what does she think m-ug or r-ug might say?

● Some common words, such as 'your', 'who' and even 'the', can't be read by sounding out. Help your child practise recognising words like these so that she can read them on sight, as whole words.

Phonic fun

Write down some of the simple story words on cards. Cut off the first letter (or the 'ch' 'sh' or 'th' beginning) from each. Help your child pair up beginnings with endings to make and read as many real or nonsense words as she can. Then cut the endings into separate letters, and play the game again.

*The text applies equally to girls and boys, but the child is referred to as 'she' throughout to avoid the use of the clumsy 'he/she'.